NANA'S
COLD
DAYS

A GROUNDWOOD BOOK

Douglas & McIntyre   Toronto   Vancouver   Berkeley

In memory of my children's nana,
Mercy Fadoa Badoe. A B

For my mother, Adassa. B J

Text copyright © 2002 Adwoa Badoe
Illustrations copyright © 2002 Bushra Junaid

Groundwood Books / Douglas & McIntyre
720 Bathurst Street, Suite 500, Toronto, Ontario M5S 2R4

Distributed in the USA by Publishers Group West
1700 Fourth Street, Berkeley, CA 94710

We acknowledge for their financial support of our publishing program the Canada Council for the Arts, the Ontario Arts Council and the Government of Canada through the Book Publishing Industry Development Program (BPIDP).

ONTARIO ARTS COUNCIL
CONSEIL DES ARTS DE L'ONTARIO

National Library of Canada Cataloguing in Publication Data
Badoe, Adwoa
Nana's cold days
ISBN 0-88899-479-6
I. Title.
PS8553.A312N35 2002   jC813'.54   C2002-900470-5
PZ7.B13865Na 2002

Bushra Junaid's illustrations are collages of painted and printed paper.
Book design by Michael Solomon
Printed and bound in China by Everbest Printing Co. Ltd.

NANA'S COLD DAYS

ADWOA BADOE

PICTURES BY

BUSHRA JUNAID

NANA stepped off the warm coast of Africa into the cold winter of North America.

"Br-r," she said. "It's too cold for living things."

With that she buried herself under three blue top sheets, three red blankets and three pink comforters, and she wouldn't come out for anyone or anything.

Papa tried, Mama tried and so did Ken and Rama. But Nana turned her face to the wall and fell fast asleep.

"Oh, dear," said Rama. "Oh, dear," said Ken.

"Oh, dear," said Papa and Mama. "We have to think of something to get our nana up."

Ken peeked through the window to see whether Nana would wake up.

"Ssh," said Rama. "You might wake her up and make her mad."

"She won't hear a thing buried under three top sheets, three blankets and three comforters," said Ken.

Nana shifted under her sheets and turned to face the door, still fast asleep.

"She will never wake up again," said Ken. "Never!"

And Nana did not wake up, not all that night and even the next day.

"I know what
will wake her up," said
Rama.

"What?" asked Ken.

"Hi-life music from
Africa. She loves that,"
said Rama.

Soon some strange
music was playing, and
a high voice was
singing something
they could not
understand.

"Isn't that cool?" asked Rama. "Doesn't it just make you want to dance?"

"No," said Ken. "I don't like it at all."

The music played for one whole hour. Although Ken liked it a little better and found his feet tapping to the drum beat, Nana was still fast asleep. She even started to snore.

"She will never wake up again," said Rama. "Never!"

"I know," said Ken suddenly. "I know what will wake her up."

"What?" asked Rama.

"Her very favorite palaver sauce and plantains. I'm going to ask Mama to make that for supper."

"Yuck!" said Rama. "I hate that stuff."

Mama peeled the plantains (which were really just cooking bananas) and boiled them in a pot with a pinch of salt. Then she

made palaver sauce with spinach fried with tomato and pepper, flavored with ginger and salted dried fish. Soon the aroma filled the air and even Rama could hardly wait for dinner.

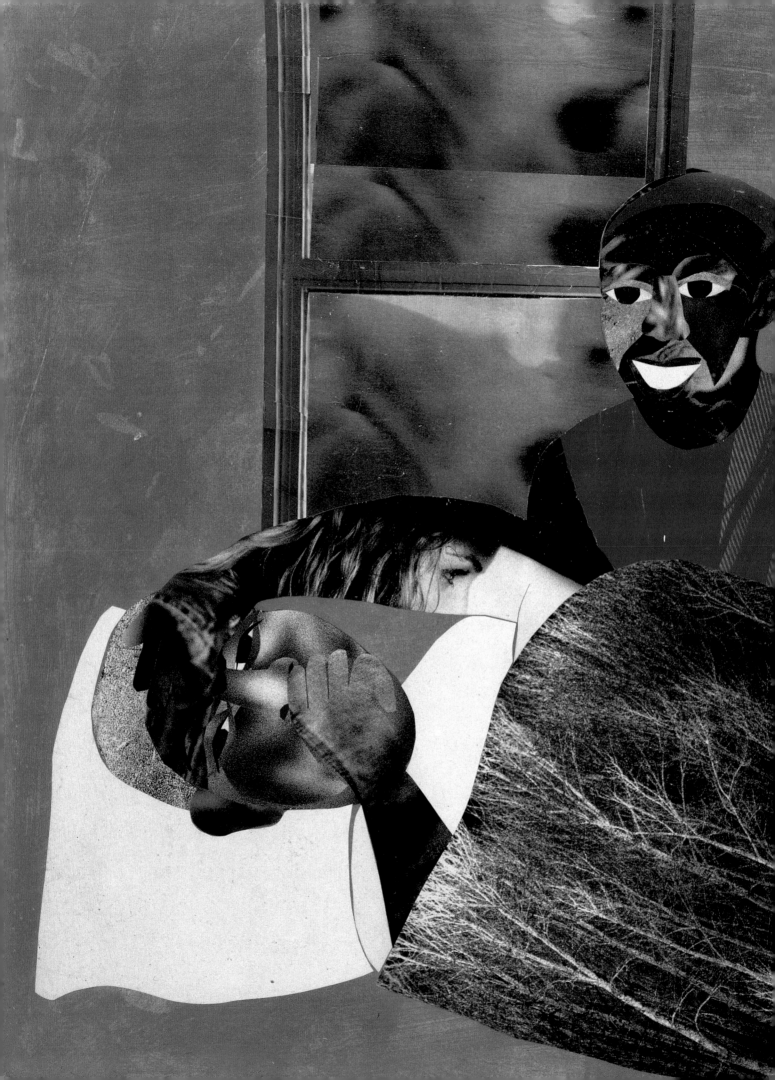

"Aatchoo, aatchoo, a-a-aatchoo!"

"Someone's caught a cold," said Mama. It was Nana.

"Oh, no," said Ken. "Double trouble! She is never going to get out of bed now."

"I bet it's from the sauce that is cooking," said Rama. "It tickles my nose, too." Everyone laughed.

Nana was too sick to get up for dinner. Instead she lay in bed and sneezed and sneezed. Poor Nana.

"Can we get you anything, Nana?" asked Papa, Mama, Rama and Ken.

"No," said Nana gruffly. "Except the doctor, maybe!" She ended with a cough that sounded like a barking dog.

"The cough sounds bad," said Rama.

"Very bad," said Ken.

The doctor came quickly to see Nana. First he took her temperature. Next he listened to her chest. Then he made her say aaaaah and looked into her throat.

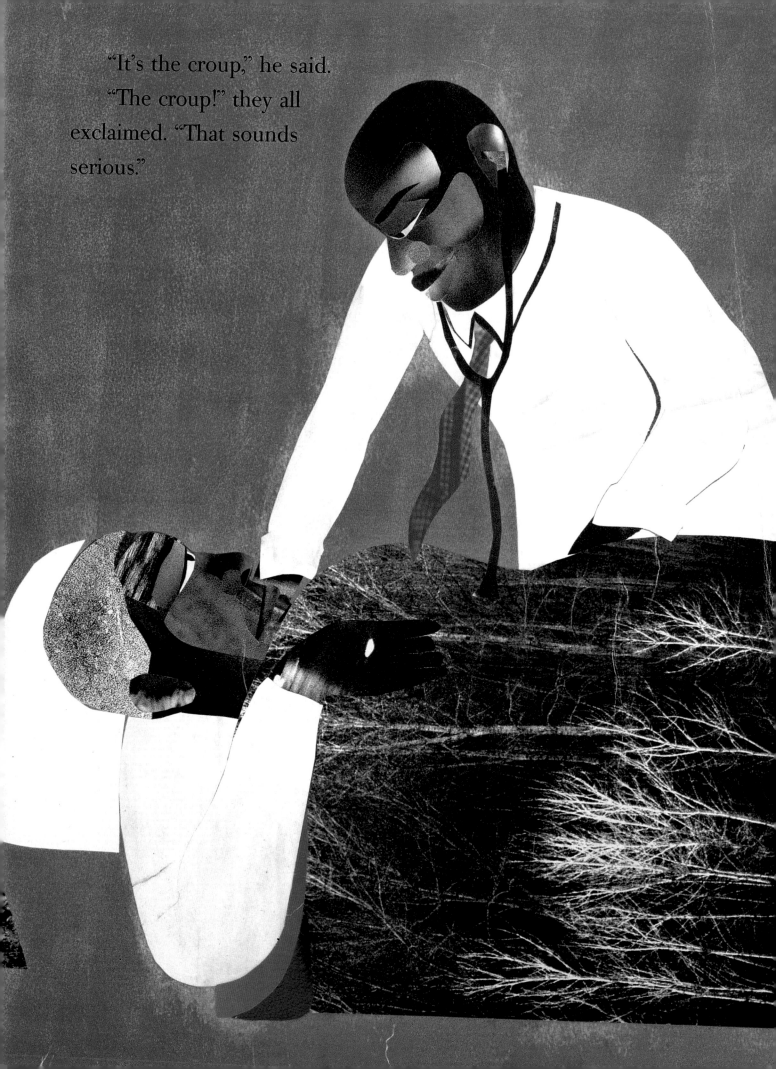

"It's the croup," he said.
"The croup!" they all
exclaimed. "That sounds
serious."

"You need to open the windows for a while and let the cold winter air in."

"Open the windows?" asked Papa. "Nana feels frozen in here already."

"The best cure for croup is the cold winter breeze," said the doctor.

They all looked at Nana huddled under three top sheets, three blankets and three comforters.

"I don't know…" said Mama.

But Nana heaved the covers to one side, marched to the windows, opened them and took in a deep breath.

Ken shivered. "B-r-r-r-r, it's freezing."

"It's c-o-o-o-o-ld," Rama's teeth chattered.

Nana smiled. "Bring me a good helping of plantain and palaver sauce and a hot cup of cocoa. I'll sit here by the window and get better quickly."

"I thought you said it was too cold for living things," said Ken.

"Living things should dress warmly for the winter," said Nana.

"Oh," said Ken.

"Oh," said Rama.

"Oh," said Papa and Mama.

"Oh!" they all exclaimed. Then they
saw that under her robe Nana was fully
clothed in a snowsuit, a hat, a scarf,
mittens and boots.

"You look ready for the Arctic," laughed Rama.

Nana laughed, too, and coughed some more.

"Now that I know that this cold air is good for some things, I'll be outside tomorrow making snow angels!"

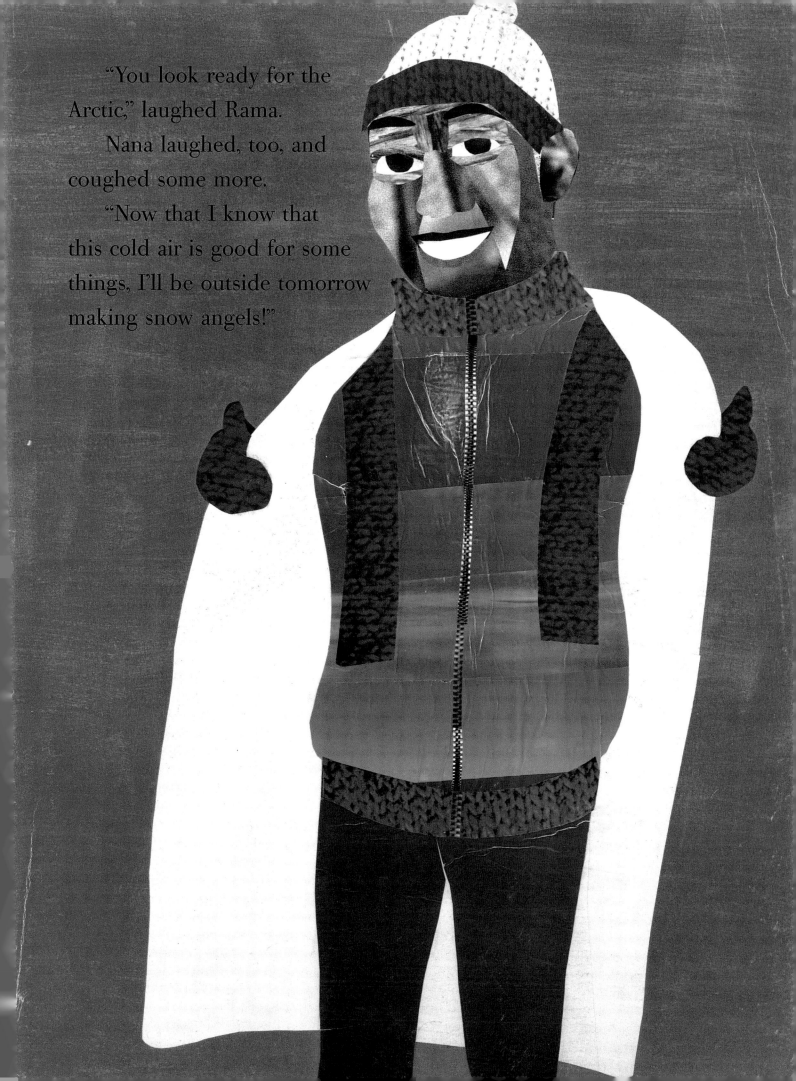